TO JESS GERBER ABZUG, MY BRAVE LITTLE WITCH —C.G.

TO KENDRA, SHAWNA, JENN, KAREN, TARA, LINDA, TRYSTAN, SARAH, OLIVE, AND SADIE—10 OF THE BUSIEST WITCHES I KNOW! —M.F.

Text copyright © 2016 by Carole Gerber
Cover art and interior illustrations copyright © 2016 by Michael Fleming

All rights reserved. Published in the United States by Doubleday,
an imprint of Random House Children's Books,
a division of Penguin Random House LLC, New York.

Doubleday and the colophon are registered trademarks of Penguin Random House LLC.

Visit us on the Web! randomhousekids.com

Educators and librarians, for a variety of teaching tools, visit us at RHTeachersLibrarians.com

Library of Congress Cataloging-in-Publication Data
Gerber, Carole.
10 busy brooms / by Carole Gerber ; illustrated by Michael Fleming. — First edition.
pages cm.
Summary: Little witches soar the sky in this cumulative Halloween counting book.
ISBN 978-0-553-53341-5 (trade) — ISBN 978-0-553-53342-2 (lib. bdg.) — ISBN 978-0-553-53343-9 (ebook)
[1. Stories in rhyme. 2. Witches—Fiction. 3. Halloween—Fiction. 4. Counting.]
I. Fleming, Michael, illustrator. II. Title. III. Title: Ten busy brooms.
PZ8.3.G297Aah 2016
[E]—dc23
2014048839

MANUFACTURED IN CHINA
10 9 8 7 6 5 4 3
First Edition

10

BUSY BROOMS

BY **CAROLE GERBER**   ILLUSTRATIONS BY **MICHAEL FLEMING**

Doubleday Books for Young Readers

1 little witch on a long, speedy broom
saw another sweeping webs from a dusty tomb.

"Come fly with me!" she called. "I've got lots of room."

2 little witches spied a third on the run.
Chasing behind was a scrawny skeleton.

"Jump on now!" they shouted. "He's a sneaky one."

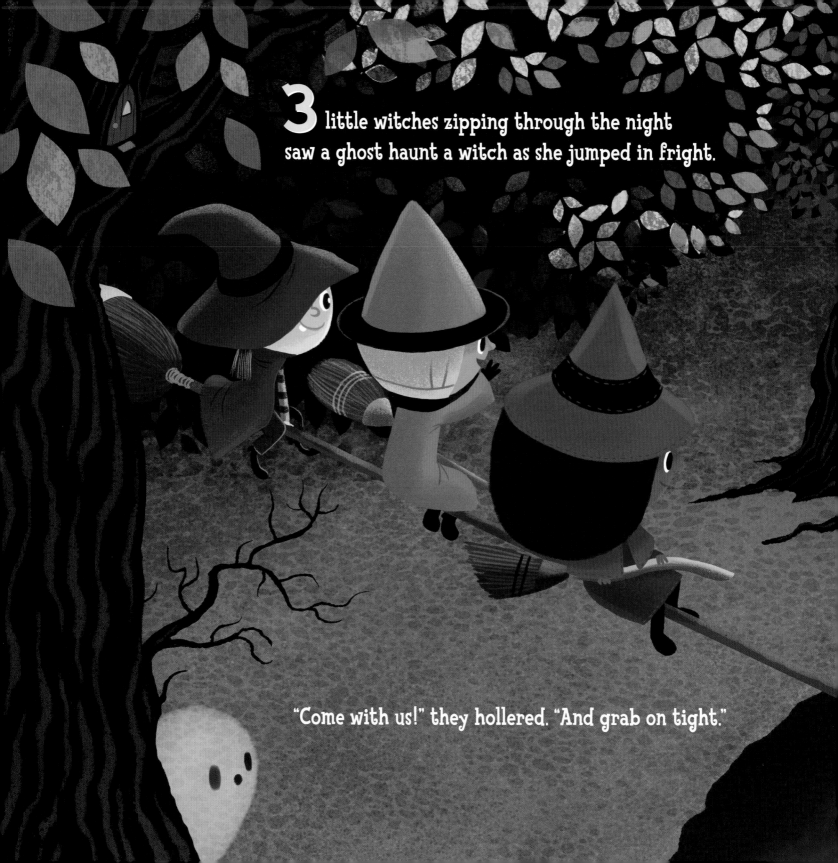

3 little witches zipping through the night
saw a ghost haunt a witch as she jumped in fright.

"Come with us!" they hollered. "And grab on tight."

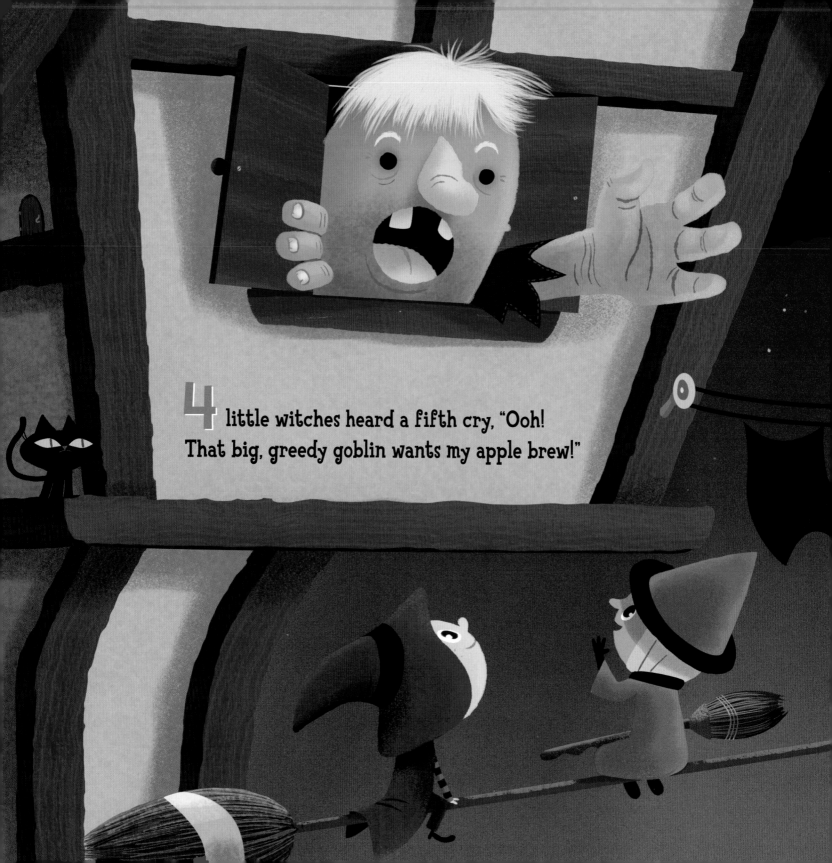

4 little witches heard a fifth cry, "Ooh!
That big, greedy goblin wants my apple brew!"

"Hop on quick!" called the witches. "Bring your brew pot, too."

5 little witches slurping supper in the sky
saw a mummy snatch another witch's pumpkin pie.

"Ride with us!" they yelled. "It's safer way up high."

6 little witches watched a werewolf prowl.
He leaped toward a seventh and let out a howl.

"Pick me up!" she begged. "His breath is really foul."

7 little witches bobbing past a bog
saw a sneaky snake slither near a witch and a frog.

"Rise and shine!" they called. "We'll lift you off that log."

8 little witches saw a big, scary bat
swoop toward a witch and her tiny white cat.

"Raise your broom!" they screeched. "We'll lift you with that."

9 little witches felt the broom dropping low.

First it **wibbled** . . .

and then **wobbled** . . .

then it fell—

OH
NO . . .

. . . near a witch eating candy,
who said, "Hello!"

"You look so real!" she cried. "Your costumes are sweet."
"We are real!" they replied, scrambling to their feet.

Then **10** little witches took off down the street . . .